Rainbo

written by Pam Holden
illustrated by Richard Hoit

She blew up one
green balloon.
Puff!

Then he blew up one
red balloon.
Puff!

He blew up two
white balloons.
Puff, puff!

Then she blew up two
pink balloons.
Puff, puff!

She blew up three
yellow balloons.
Puff, puff, puff!

Then he blew up three blue balloons.
Puff, puff, puff!

He blew up four
green balloons.
Puff, puff, puff, puff!

Then she blew up four red balloons.
Puff, puff, puff, puff!

He blew up five
orange balloons.
Puff, puff, puff, puff, puff!

Then she blew up
five purple balloons.
Puff, puff, puff, puff, puff!

He blew up six blue balloons.
Puff, puff, puff,
puff, puff, puff!

Then she blew up six yellow balloons. Puff, puff, puff, puff, puff, puff!

She blew up seven purple balloons. Puff, puff, puff, puff, puff, puff, puff!

Then he blew up seven white balloons. Puff, puff, puff, puff, puff, puff, puff!

They blew up too
many balloons!
Help!   Help!   Help!